Be Fair and Share!

By Maria Maysen

Illustrated by
Laura Logan

SCHOLASTIC INC.

For Wren and Desmond, who teach me about sharing every day.
—M.M.

For Grant, Liam & Hudson, with love
—L.L.

Text copyright © 2015 by Maria Maysen
Illustrations copyright © 2015 by Laura Logan

10 9 8 7 6 5 4 3 2 1   15 16 17 18 19

ISBN 978-0-545-89046-5

Printed in the U.S.A.   40
First printing 2015

Today is a special day for Cubby!

Cubby's friend Monkey is coming over to play after school.

Cubby wakes up early and pulls out all his favorite toys.

"That's a lot of toys!" says his daddy.

"I know!" says Cubby. "Monkey and I are going to play with them today after school!"

Cubby carefully lines up his Rocket Blaster, Rexi the dinosaur, the Snowball Shaker, the Superhero Flyer, and his most favorite toy of all: Woof the stuffed wolf.

Then it's time to go to school!

"Circle time today is all about sharing," says Ms. Elephant. "What are some things you can do when two friends want to play with the same toy at school?"

Cheetah says, "Whoever gets to the toy the fastest gets it first!"

Giraffe says, "But after that, the friends can take turns!"

"Or they can play with it at the same time!"

Hippo and Rhino say together.

"Great ideas!" says Ms. Elephant. "Toys at school are for everyone, and that means you need to be fair and share! But what if it's your own, very special toy?"

"I might not want to share my Lovey Blankie," says Monkey.

"And I wouldn't want to share my Fuzzy Bunny," says Tiger.

"I think it's okay if you don't want to share a very special toy," says Ms. Elephant. "Cubby, is there one toy that you might not want to share?"

A a

Cubby thinks, but he isn't sure he can choose just one.

When pickup time comes, Cubby's daddy walks Cubby and Monkey home and makes them a yummy snack.

Then it is time to play
in Cubby's room!

"This is my Rexi the dinosaur," Cubby says. "He roars when you press the button on his tail."

"I have one of those at home," says Monkey. "What's that one?"

"This is my favorite, Woof," Cubby says, picking up Woof. "He looks just like a real wolf."

"Cool!" says Monkey. He reaches for the stuffed wolf.

Cubby holds Woof behind his back. "He likes to stay on the shelf," he says, and puts Woof back.

"Whoa," says Monkey, picking up a toy.
"Oh," says Cubby. "That's my Rocket Blaster."

"Cool! Can we play with it?"

"Well . . . ," Cubby says. "I guess so."

Monkey sets the toy down on the floor and presses the red button. The rocket flies into the air!

"WHOA!" Monkey yells. "It goes so high! Let's try it again."

But Cubby doesn't like the way Monkey plays with the blaster. "No, that's enough," Cubby says, and he puts the toy back on the shelf.

"How is it going, kids?" Cubby's daddy asks.

"Okay," Monkey says. But he doesn't look okay.

"Cubby?" his daddy asks. "Are you sharing your toys?"

Cubby looks down at his furry toes. "I don't want to share."

"He doesn't want to share," Monkey agrees.

"I see," says Cubby's daddy, and he takes Cubby by the hand into the hallway for a chat.

"He wants to play with all of my special toys!" Cubby says, pouting.

"It's important to *be fair and share* when you have a friend come over to play," Cubby's daddy tells him. "But if you have a special toy that you want to put away, that's okay, too."

"Okay," says Cubby. Then he has an idea!

Into the closet goes Rexi. Into the closet goes Woof. Into the closet goes the Rocket Blaster, the Snowball Shaker, and the Superhero Flyer, too.

Cubby feels better. But Monkey is sad. There are no toys to play with!

"Hmm," says Cubby's daddy when he pokes his head into the bedroom again.

Once again, he takes Cubby gently by the paw into the hallway for a chat.

"Do you think Monkey is having fun on this playdate?"

"No," Cubby says quietly.

"Do you think you would like being on a playdate where your friend wouldn't share *any* of his toys?"

"No," says Cubby again.

"Well, is there anything you think you could do to make this playdate fun for both of you?"

Cubby thinks for a minute, and then he says, "Be fair and share!"

Out of the closet comes the Superhero Flyer. Out comes the Rocket Blaster, the Snowball Shaker, and out comes Rexi. But Woof stays in. Monkey claps his paws and shouts, "Hooray!"

"Hey, let's take turns pressing the red button on the Rocket Blaster!" Cubby says.

"Yay!" says Monkey. "Then can we see which goes higher, the Rocket Blaster or the Superhero Flyer?"

"Great idea!" says Cubby.

All afternoon, the two friends laugh, play . . .

. . . and share.